THE GIFT OF A
TRAVELER

BY WENDY MATTHEWS
PICTURES BY ROBERT VAN NUTT

BridgeWater Paperback

In memory of Robin Tate, who first encouraged me to write.
His spirit lives on in these words.
And with thanks to the group:
Beryl Afton, Tom McKean, Nigel Pugh, Marcia Savin,
and Debbie Schecter.

W.M.

To the memory of my father,
for whom there were no strangers,
just friends he hadn't yet met.

R.V.N.

Text copyright © 1995 by Wendy Matthews.
Illustrations copyright © 1995 by Robert Van Nutt.
Designed by Leslie Bauman.
Published by BridgeWater Paperback, an imprint and
trademark of Troll Communications L.L.C.

First published in hardcover by BridgeWater Books.

First paperback edition 1996.

Printed in the United States of America.

10 9 8 7 6 5 4 3 2 1

Library of Congress Cataloging-in-Publication Data

Matthews, Wendy
The gift of a traveler / by Wendy Matthews;
pictures by Robert Van Nutt.

p. cm

Summary: Seven-year-old Christine spends Christmas Eve helping
her great-grandmother decorate her tree and sharing the story of a
very special ornament that came from Romania many years before.

ISBN 0-8167-3656-1 (lib.) ISBN 0-8167-3657-X (pbk.)

[1. Christmas—Fiction. 2. Great-grandmothers—Fiction.
3. Romania—Fiction.] I. Van Nutt, Robert, ill. II. Title.
PZ7.M4345Gi   1995   [E]--dc20   94-35307

THE OLD WOMAN

From out of the gloom, a long, bony finger pointed.

"Here?"

The old woman nodded slowly as the little girl carefully placed the last ornament on the proper branch. It was Christmas Eve.

Christine had shown each ornament to her great-grandmother as she took it from its tissue-lined box. The tissue paper was soft and very wrinkled, not like the tissue her mother had at home for wrapping presents. Christine wished she were home now instead of being stuck here with her great-grandmother.

"Chrissy, I have so much to do today," her mother had said. "Spend the day with Great-grandma. She needs help decorating her tree, and she's lonely now that Great-grandpa's gone."

"But I want to help you," Christine had replied. "I want to bake cookies."

"The biggest help you can be is to go to Great-grandma's. She's really not so scary when you know her." But Great-grandma was from a faraway country and a distant time. And to Christine, who was only seven, that seemed a little scary.

Christine ran her fingers over the wrinkly tissue paper. It had tiny flecks of shiny color and was soft and made no sound. The little boxes the decorations had been packed in had no words on them, just lovely patterns and colors. Not at all like the cardboard and cellophane boxes at home.

"These are pretty." Bravely, Christine held up one of the little boxes.

"They are from my home, from Romania. You know where Romania is?" The old woman sat in her big chair in the corner, shrouded in darkness.

Christine shook her head. She was thinking about whether she could go home now that the tree was decorated. She couldn't imagine what else she and her great-grandmother would do together. There were no toys here and the old woman didn't talk much.

"Um, I guess it's time I was going," said Christine.

"Not finished yet." The voice came from the darkness. "There is something else. You will bring it for me. Come here."

Christine had never dared approach her great-grandmother's chair before. Her mother had told her that Great-grandma's old eyes worked better in the half-light. But Christine wished she could see the old woman's face.

"Come here."

The voice sounded kind. Christine crept closer and saw that her great-grandmother was smiling. The old woman reached into a pocket in the side of her rough woolen dress and pulled out a bunch of tiny keys. She selected one carefully.

"This one. Look."

The old finger pointed again, this time at an enormous dark wooden cupboard against the far wall. "Open the door on the right."

Christine wondered how such a dainty key could go with such a gigantic piece of furniture. It went almost to the ceiling and had birds and flowers carved on it.

The huge old door swung open easily. Inside were row after row of small drawers, each with a tiny lock and each carved with an image. Each carving seemed to tell a story. The smell of the old wood was strong and comforting.

"Third row from the bottom," said Great-grandma.

Christine counted up—one, two, three.

"Now two from the right." One, two.

On the drawer was a carving of a man playing a guitar. He was sitting beside a tree, and he wore a coat covered with stars.

"Open the drawer."

The little key turned in the lock. In the drawer lay something wrapped in soft, shiny tissue.

"Bring it here."

Christine carefully carried the package to her great-grandmother's chair.

"This is the most precious thing that I have. Would you like to see it?"

Christine nodded as she watched the old, steady fingers unwrap the tissue. Inside was an ornament, different from any she had ever seen.

"I have had this ever since I was a child. It could be there is magic in it."

Christine looked at her great-grandmother, wide-eyed. "Really? Where did you get it?"

"Would you like to hear the story?"

Christine nodded.

"It takes place in Romania, where I was born, in a place with mountains and forests. It was Christmas Eve of the year 1910, when I was seven years old, like you. . . ."

Christine closed her eyes and let the old woman's voice wash over her, taking her into another time and place.

ANICA'S STORY

We lived in a small cottage on the side of a mountain, far from villages or other people. We kept a farm, and around our few tilled fields were rocky outcroppings and thick forests. Our cottage had a steeply pitched roof with eaves hung low to protect against the deep snows of winter. Inside were only three rooms.

Everyone in my family—my parents, brother, two sisters, and I—had work to do around the farm. I was the youngest, so I looked after the chickens. In winter, when the days were short, we would work until dark fell. Then we would hurry inside to sit by the fire and look at books. This was our school. We lived too far away from any village to go to school with other children, so we learned everything from our parents and our books.

On this particular day, Christmas Eve, we finished our chores early, and instead of doing our schoolwork we children went to the forest with our father to cut down a Christmas tree. It was our family's custom on Christmas Eve that each of us children presented to the tree ă pom de Crăciún, an ornament we had made ourselves. I planned to make mine out of pinecones, but I still needed to collect a few more, especially a perfect one for the center.

Snow was falling as we brought the tree home. It was beginning to get dark, and the huge pines looked black against the snowy sky. Under their canopy all was silent, apart from the crunch of my family's boots in the deep snow and the swoosh of the sled carrying our tree.

My father and brother pulled the sled along, while my two sisters ran ahead. I was supposed to walk at the back to make sure the tree stayed on the sled. I had been gathering pinecones as we walked, and now I saw an almost perfect one—the very one I'd dreamed of—and ran off to collect it. I dashed through the trees to where I'd seen it, but I couldn't find it. Maybe it was on a different tree? As I searched for it, I heard my father's voice.

"Hurry up, Anica, we don't want a wolf to get you," he called. There were many wolves in the mountains and forests around the farm, and often I could hear them howling in the night. If the moon was full, I would sometimes run to the bedroom window and see them ringing the farm, howling, howling. The colder it became, the closer in they came, and sometimes a wolf would take one of the farm animals. I would cover my ears and climb back into the safety of the bed I shared with my sisters.

When my father spoke, I ran to catch up, but the snow was thick and I slipped and fell. I could feel the cold dampness of the snow pressing against my chest like a suffocating cloud as I lay on the ground. I could also sense eyes upon me, even though my family was out of sight. I turned my head and peered into the darkening woods and saw a shape, a movement, a flash of gray fur. A wolf! My heart pounding, I struggled to get up, but my feet would not grip the slippery surface. The cold ground pulled me back into its grasp.

"Father!" I cried.

No reply.

I could feel something moving closer. As I heard the snow crunch, I squeezed my eyes shut. The snow against my right cheek made me numb with cold, while hot breath against my left sent a wave of terror through me. I tried to call out again; then I must have fainted.

Something was licking my face. I was very cold. I opened my eyes and saw the muzzle and the blue eyes of a wolf.

"Don't be afraid, little one," said a deep voice. "Sasha won't hurt you. She is my friend."

Beyond the wolf's blue eyes, I could see a curious pair of boots. They were dyed red and green, not brown like mine. Above the boots was a fur-lined coat that came all the way down to the ground. The outside was embroidered with thousands of tiny stars.

"Come, give me your hand, little one," said the voice.

A big hand in a fur glove pulled me to my feet. The man knelt before me. He wore a pointed fur-lined hat, and over his shoulder was slung an oddly shaped leather bag. I looked into his face; he was different from anyone I had ever seen. He had dark skin, black eyes, and a dark beard. He wore a large gold earring in his right ear. Then he smiled, and his teeth were whiter than snow.

"Who are you?" I asked.

"I am a *țigan*," he replied. "A traveler. Some call me a gypsy."

I eyed the wolf warily. Even sitting down, she was almost taller than I was. She looked me over, then gracefully lifted her paw and offered it to me. I stared.

"She is greeting you," said the traveler.

Sasha waited patiently, her paw outstretched. Slowly, I reached out and grasped it. I was holding the paw of a wolf!

Suddenly, I turned in the direction my family had gone. It was almost dark and they were nowhere in sight. I was all alone in the dark forest with a wolf and a stranger.

"My family is gone!" I said, and burst into tears.

"No need to weep, little one," said the *țigan*. "Your father is coming to find you. He has a lantern. I can see him."

I looked all around but could see no light. "Where?" I said.

"He has just left your cottage and is entering the forest," said the traveler. "Come, we will go to meet him. Sasha will lead us."

Once again, the man offered me his big gloved hand and I took it in mine. We walked behind Sasha through the dark forest. Questions ran through my head: How could this man see in the dark all the way to our cottage? What was he doing in the forest as night fell? It was too cold to sleep outside.

"Where do you live?" I asked.

"I am a traveler," he replied.

"But where do you sleep?"

"Wherever I may."

Just then, a pinprick of light shone through the trees.

"Father!" I cried joyously, and ran toward the light. "*Tată*!" I threw my arms around him.

"Anica! I'm glad you're safe," my father murmured, holding me tightly. Then his voice grew stern and, holding me at arm's length, he shook me a little. "What happened? You must stay with me when we're in the forest."

I hung my head. "I'm sorry, Father. I fell in the snow while looking for pinecones. I called you, but you didn't hear me."

My excitement quickly returned. "A man saved me. He has a friend called Sasha who's a wolf, and he doesn't have a home. Come meet him!" I said breathlessly. Suddenly, I was very proud of my new friend. I turned back toward the dark forest. "*Țigan*!" I called.

I could see my father's lantern reflected in two sets of eyes as the man and the wolf approached. The traveler had his hand on Sasha's head.

"Thank you, friend, for bringing my daughter to safety," said my father politely. Still, I could see that the strange man made him uneasy.

Sasha sat down in front of my father and gracefully lifted her paw as she had done for me.

"Sasha is greeting you," said the traveler. "You have nothing to fear from her. She is quite tame."

Uncertainly, my father took the wolf's paw.

"The little one had a fright, but she is well. Now she is cold and should be brought before a fire." As the traveler said this, I realized that my teeth were chattering and my bones were aching with chill.

My father smiled cautiously. "Thank you again, friend," he said, turning to go, "and merry Christmas. *Sărbători fericite!*"

"Wait!" I said, as my father led me away. I turned back to the traveler. "If you don't have a home, where do you go for Christmas?"

"Wherever I may," he replied.

I looked at my father, then at the traveler. "Where will you go tonight?"

The traveler didn't reply.

"Will you come to our house?" I blurted out all at once.

There was silence for a moment while we stood in the lantern's glow under the dark pines. Finally, my father spoke.

"Yes," he said hesitantly, "will you come and share our Christmas?"

"I would be most grateful," said the traveler, and together we headed back to our cottage.

❄   ❄   ❄

My mother held out her arms in greeting as we approached, although I could see she was wary. No one ever came to our cottage, especially not a curiously clad man and a wolf. The only time we saw other people was on our monthly trip to the market in Toplița, the nearest town.

"Thank you, *mulțumesc*, for your hospitality," said the traveler as he strode into our cottage. Sasha sat in front of my mother and offered her paw. My mother shook her head in disbelief; my brother and sisters were pressed against the back wall of the room, staring.

"Her name is Sasha and she's his friend," I said, bravely stroking the wolf's ears. I heard my sister Sofia gasp. "You can shake her paw. She won't harm you."

My mother laughed nervously, then reached out and lightly touched the wolf's paw.

"Perhaps the wolf—Sasha—should stay outside," said my father, watching my mother's face.

"No, no, she'll freeze," I said, this time putting my arm around Sasha's neck. Sofia gasped again.

"She can stay inside," said my mother, smiling at me and the big gray wolf. "However, tonight," she said, turning to the traveler, "I'm very sorry, but you'll have to sleep in the stable. We have no extra beds or, indeed, any room in this tiny cottage for two more to sleep."

"Thank you," said the traveler. "The stable is excellent. Now we must get the little one warm." And he lifted me up and placed me in front of the fire.

That evening at our traditional Christmas Eve dinner, I could see that my family was uncomfortable. My parents tried to make the *țigan* feel welcome, but they were unused to company. My two sisters sat in awed silence, while my brother tried to overcome his shyness and join in the conversation. Sasha ate scraps under the table.

Little by little, my mysterious new friend put the family at ease by telling us fantastic stories of his travels to faraway places. They were the most wonderful stories we children had ever heard, and I remember them still.

There were tales of sea monsters and magic carpets, and of strange deserts where it never snowed and nothing ever grew. One of the tales was about the church domes and steeples in Bucharest. The traveler told us how, if you climbed to the top of the tallest one on a particular day, you could see your future laid out before you.

"You, little one, could see all the places you will travel to," said the traveler.

"Me?" I said. I thought that going to Toplița was a long trip.

"You will see those steeples and even greater wonders, little one. You will be a traveler, too."

After dinner came my favorite part—decorating the tree. Most of our ornaments were homemade, and each year we children made new ones. But this year I had not. The pinecones I had collected lay on the snowy forest floor where I dropped them when I fell.

While we hung the pretty trinkets on the tree, the traveler played on a *chitară,* a beautifully carved guitar, and sang in a language we did not know. Sasha sat by the fire, warming herself, and sometimes I would stroke her. The fur on her stomach was light beige and soft, and she had unusual black markings that looked almost like a saddle across the gray fur of her back. When I stroked her belly, she licked me.

After the tree had been decorated, my mother put candles on many of its branches. This was always the best part of the evening. My father would light all the candles, making the room glow with a soft yellow light. Then we children would add the new ornaments we had made that year. We always went in order of age, and I was dreading my turn.

"Petrachi, you first," said my father. "Show us what you have made."

My brother, the eldest, carefully unwrapped a deer fashioned from dozens of tiny twigs woven together. Bathed in the candle glow, he solemnly carried it around the room for all to see.

"Oh Petrachi," sighed my mother, "this is most beautiful." She turned to the *ţigan.* "Every year, his work gets better. Soon, no one will be able to match it."

"His hands are nimble," said the traveler, flashing his white-toothed smile at my brother. Even in the dim candlelight, I could see Petrachi blush as he hung his deer on the tree.

"Now you, Sofia," said my father.

Sofia looked around nervously. She was the quietest of us, and she was not happy that we had a wolf and a stranger in the house. From her apron pocket, she pulled a circle of wood painted in bright colors. Shyly, she showed it to us.

"It is lovely, *iubita,*" said my father.

Sasha got up from her warm spot in front of the fire and walked over to Sofia. Sofia stood stock-still, frozen in fear, as Sasha approached. The wolf inspected Sofia's ornament, then nuzzled her head against my sister's side. Sofia gradually began to melt, and to giggle quietly as the big gray wolf made friends with her.

"And now for Elena."

Elena wasn't much for handicrafts; she usually preferred to run around outside and play. I was hoping that she, too, would not have an ornament for this year's tree. But she surprised us all and brought out a little figure dressed in white.

"It's an angel," she announced proudly. "Mother taught me how to sew this year."

"And she's quite good at it, for a beginner," said my mother, beaming. Everyone laughed and commented on Elena's new talent.

After the angel was hung on the tree, my family and our guests all turned and looked at me.

"And what have you made, Anica?"

I studied the toes of my old brown boots.

"Anica? You must answer when you're spoken to," said my father.

I looked at him sadly and shook my head.

"You have nothing to give our tree?"

"I was going to make something out of pinecones, but I dropped them when I fell." The room was silent for a moment.

"I see. Well, never mind," said my father.

I looked at the traveler. He wasn't smiling at me now; he looked very solemn. My friend, my *prieten,* must be very disappointed in me. I had nothing to give.

❄   ❄   ❄

We always stayed up late on Christmas Eve. Outside, the snow was falling thickly and the wind roared down the mountainside. Inside, though, we were gathered around the glowing tree, next to the warm fireplace, sipping hot milk and eating *cozonac*—sweet bread with raisins, nuts, and honey.

The traveler told more fabulous tales, and we sang along as he played some songs we all knew on his *chitară.* My family and he seemed comfortable together now. But throughout it all, I felt sad. I could not forget that I had not made an ornament.

"Our little Anica is tired from her adventures in the forest, aren't you, *dragostea mea,*" said my mother, stroking my hair.

I said nothing. My special friend the *țigan* was here and I had nothing to give our tree. What must he think of me?

Then it was time for bed. The snow had stopped and my father prepared to lead the traveler and Sasha to the stable where they would sleep. My mother found plenty of warm blankets for them, and the traveler assured us they would be quite comfortable.

"Good night, *Ţigan*," I said. "Tomorrow we can all play in the snow." I hoped that he and Sasha were still my friends.

He smiled at me and gently took my hand. "Good night, little one. Do not be sad. You have given much. You have given me friendship and trust and companionship. *La revedere!*"

Sasha licked me good night and they followed my father through the deep snow to the stable.

That night, I had dreams of huge dark pinecones falling from my hands and the breath of a wolf on my cheek.

❄ ❄ ❄

The next morning was crisp and blue and clear. As I opened my eyes, I was blinded by a ray of bright sunlight streaming across the bed where I and my sisters slept. It illuminated something in my outstretched hand. Whatever it was glowed so brightly that I could barely look at it.

Slowly, I closed my fingers around it. It felt like wood, with pointy ends and bits sticking out. I pulled my arm under the covers and ducked my head into the darkness of the bed. The object filled the bed with light, but I could look at it now.

Although it was only made of carved and painted wood, it glowed. It seemed very delicate, but I could tell by touching it that it was also very strong. The ends were pointed, carved to look like the church steeples in Bucharest that I had seen in pictures, but the heart of it was what amazed me most. Snowflake upon snowflake, each slightly different in color and shape, were set one inside the other. In the very center was a simple pinecone.

It was a Christmas tree ornament and I knew it was a gift from the traveler. I lay there under the covers for a long time, gazing at the beautiful object, and was filled with wonder, sadness, and joy.

Suddenly, I sat up. I must thank my friend! My sisters were still sleeping, but I could hear sounds coming from downstairs. I jumped out of bed, pulled on my clothes, and ran down. My father was at the hearth, starting up a fire.

"Merry Christmas, *Tătic*!" I said gaily.

He caught me in his arms and gave me a big hug. "*Sărbători fericite, iubita*," he said. "Merry Christmas, sweetheart."

"Look! Look what the traveler gave me! Now I have something to give our tree." I held out the glowing ornament for my father to see.

"Where did you get this?" he asked.

"I told you! The *țigan* gave it to me. When I woke up, it was in my hand. Where is he? I want to say thank you."

"I haven't seen him today. Perhaps he is still out in the stable." My father stared at me. "Are you sure he didn't give it to you last night?"

"No! It was in my hand when I woke. He must have brought it to me just this morning."

"How did he get into the cottage?" asked my father. "The door is barred."

He strode over to the door to demonstrate. The door was indeed barred. My father lifted out of its slots the heavy board that held the door shut. He glanced outside.

"No one has been to the cottage door this morning," he said. "Look at the footprints."

I ran to the door and gazed at the dazzling blue and white of that Christmas morning.

"See?" my father said. "Three sets of footprints leading to the stable—mine, the traveler's, and Sasha's—and one coming back—mine."

I gasped. My father was right. How had the traveler delivered my beautiful gift to me?

Without a coat and still clutching my treasure to my chest, I ran through the snow to the stable and flung open the door.

The stable was cold. There was no one there. In a corner stood the pile of blankets, untouched, and the lamp that my father had carried out for our visitor, unlit. My friend was gone.

My father walked up behind me and surveyed the scene.

"Where did he go?" I said, tears starting to flow down my cheeks.

"He didn't even sleep here," said my father. "Who knows where he went? If he slept outside last night, he would have frozen to death, but there isn't anywhere else for him to go for miles around."

The tears flowed faster at the thought of my friend and his gentle wolf freezing to death in the snow. Then I felt a warmth against my chest. "He didn't freeze," I said. I looked down at my glowing ornament. It was sending warmth all through me now. "He has magic with him."

I never saw the traveler again. But once, a few years later, when I was in the forest collecting kindling with my mother, I saw a flash of gray fur through the trees. I felt frightened until the wolf ran out into a clearing up ahead and turned to look at us. There was something familiar about the black markings on its back.

"Sasha?" I said.

The wolf ran a few steps closer, and I could see its intelligent blue eyes.

"Sasha!" I cried joyfully, and started to move toward her.

She bowed her head, as if in greeting, then turned and ran off into the trees.

THE GIFT

"I have always kept this ornament with me," said the old woman. "First in the mountains, then in town after I was married, then when we went to Bucharest. When we left Romania to come to America, we were running away and could not bring many things with us. My husband was angry with me, but I would not leave it."

Christine looked down at the ornament nestled in her lap. It glowed softly. "I would never leave it either."

She thought for a moment about the story her great-grandmother had just told her. "What the traveler said was true. You're a traveler, too."

"A țigan . . ." The old woman looked straight ahead. "You know how old I am? I am more than ninety years old. There are not many years left. I want you to love this the way I have. I want you to have this."

Christine looked at her great-grandmother, climbed into the old woman's chair, and threw her arms around her neck. "No, Great-grandma. You must keep it."

"I will keep it here with me, but it is yours now. Every year you will come and hang it on my tree. And one day you will hang it on yours."

They sat together in the old woman's chair for a long time, looking at the magical ornament. The years had muted its glow to that of soft candlelight. Then Christine helped her great-grandmother Anica from her chair, and slowly they made their way to the tree. They studied the tree for some time, choosing the very best spot. And, together, the old woman and the little girl placed the ornament among the softly scented pine needles, where it belonged.